Here's That Kitten

by Maria Polushkin

illustrated by Betsy Lewin

Bradbury Press • New York

Bradbury Press
An Affiliate of Macmillan, Inc.
866 Third Avenue, New York, NY 10022
Collier Macmillan Canada, Inc.

The text of this book is set in ITC Clearface.
The illustrations are rendered in watercolor and black ink.
Typography by Julie Quan

Printed and bound in the United States of America
First Edition

10 9 8 7 6 5 4 3 2 1

LIBRARY OF CONGRESS CATALOGING-IN-PUBLICATION DATA
Polushkin, Maria.
    Here's that kitten / by Maria Polushkin; illustrated by
Betsy Lewin. — 1st ed.
        p.   cm.
    Summary: A kitten creates havoc in the house knocking
over things, climbing onto the roof, and hiding in the
chimney and then spreading soot everywhere before
charming the family with its cuteness.
    ISBN 0-02-774741-7
    [1. Cats—Fiction.]   I. Lewin, Betsy, ill.   II. Title.
PZ7.P7695He   1990
[E]—dc 19   89-829   CIP   AC

Kitten hated cleaning day.
Trouble found him everywhere.

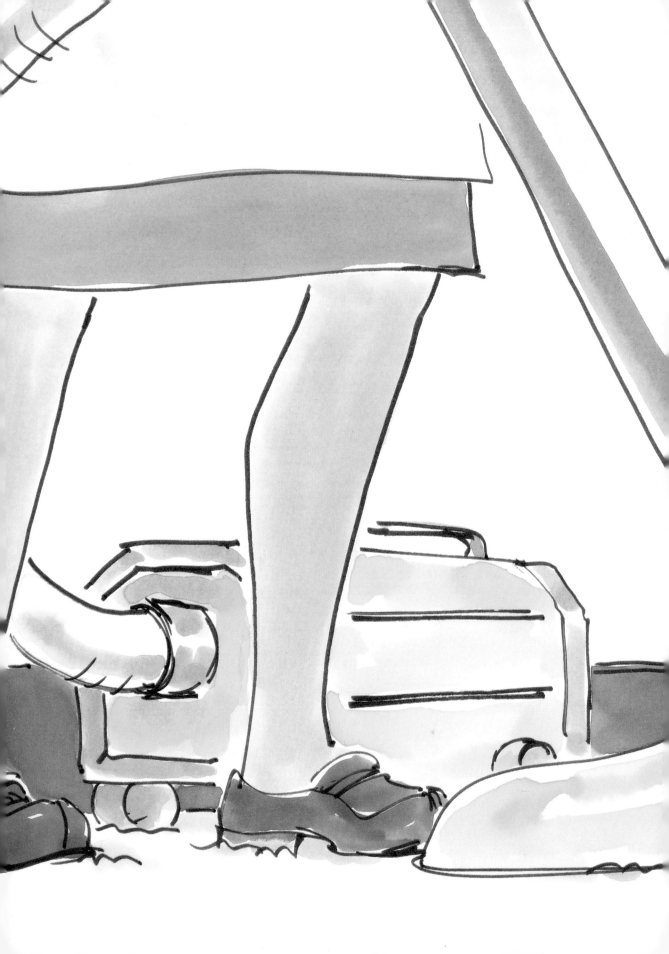

The vacuum cleaner roared
at him. *Whoosh!*

Brooms swept him. *Scat!*

Mops attacked him. *Splash!*

Sprays hissed at him. *Splat!*

Dusters chased him.
Shoo!

Only one room was safe.

Oh no! Drat that kitten.

Oh no! Hold that kitten.

Oh no! Watch that kitten.

Oh no! Where's that kitten?

Oh no! Stop that kitten!

Oh no! Catch that kitten.

Oh no! Wash that kitten.

Oh no! Dry that kitten.

Please stay out of
trouble, Kitten.

Just be good and
take a nap, Kitten.

Oh no! Here's that kitten!

Stay and have
some milk, Kitten.

That's a good kitten!